The Greatest Fall from Grace

Jessy King

iUniverse, Inc.
Bloomington

The Greatest Fall from Grace

iUniverse books may be ordered through booksellers or by contacting:

iUniverse
1663 Liberty Drive
Bloomington, IN 47403
www.iuniverse.com
1-800-Authors (1-800-288-4677)

ISBN: 978-1-4759-6170-6 (sc)
ISBN: 978-1-4759-6168-3 (e)
ISBN: 978-1-4759-6169-0 (dj)

Library of Congress Control Number: 2012921567

Printed in the United States of America

iUniverse rev. date: 11/14/2012

Dedication

This book is dedicated to all the people who have touched my life in some way. To all my family, friends, and coworkers, former and current, you have helped shape the person I am today. I am a better person because of what you have taught me. Thank you from the bottom of my heart. You will always be in my thoughts.

Contents

Prologue: In the Beginning

In the beginning, there was an Almighty Power, known by the name *the Lord God, his royal majesty.* His greatest creation, Lucifer, stood on his right. Lucifer was the Almighty's go-to divine servant. Whatever the Almighty wanted, Lucifer was pleased to do. After one special dawn over heaven;

THE LORD: Lucifer, I wish to create two heavens, one where heavenly hosts may reside and a second that will be sanctuary for me.

And so it came to pass, and there were two heavens. The Lord saw that it was good and was pleased. Nightfall came, and dawn followed the next day.

THE LORD: Lucifer, I want there to be light, one that shall rise at dawn and a second that shall rise at dusk.

And so there were two types of light. One was called sun, and one was called moon. The Lord saw it was good and was pleased. Nightfall came, and dawn the next day.

THE LORD: Lucifer, I want there to be many different seas, and out of these seas, I want land to surface.

And so it was; there were seas of all types, and land above them. The Lord saw it was good and was pleased. Nightfall came, and dawn the next day.

THE LORD: Lucifer, I want there to be flora of every type in both the land and the sea, multiplied ten million times ten. I want there to be fauna of every type in both the land and the sea, also multiplied ten million times ten.

And so it came to pass. Fauna and flora of every type filled the land and the seas. The Lord saw that it was good and was pleased. Nightfall came, and dawn the next day.

THE LORD: Lucifer, I want there to be a garden in the land of Eden. I want it to hold eternal life and knowledge.

And so a garden was established in the land of Eden. The Lord saw that it was good and was pleased. Nightfall came, and dawn the next day.

THE LORD: Lucifer, days in this realm come in sevens. Today, the day of proclamation, I shall establish the laws of Eden. At the end of every six days, there shall be one day of reverence; I shall call it my Sabbath. In the land of Eden, never once shall another god stand before me. Never once shall my name be spoken in vain. We shall love our mother earth and father for all time. Never once shall false words be spoken. Never once shall life be ended by any hand but mine. Never once shall food be removed improperly. Random fornication will not occur. And no one shall covet another's possessions.

And so it was. The Lord's laws were cemented into the fabric of this new realm. Nightfall came, and dawn came on the next day. The Lord saw what he had done and was pleased. Lucifer took the holy scrolls that recorded the Lord's words and placed them in a tabernacle for all eternity.

Chapter 1: A New Creation

Part 1

The Lord and Lucifer are sitting in heaven, admiring the Lord's creation. However, the Lord seems to be bothered about something.

THE LORD: Lucifer, something is missing in my garden.

LUCIFER: What is missing, my Lord?

THE LORD: A statue in my image.

LUCIFER: I will tell the angels to collect the best clay for making a statue of your majesty.

And so every angel in heaven collects clay for the Lord, who works all night on his statue. The Lord places the statue underneath the Tree of Life and Knowledge. Sleeping at its feet are three angels, the guardians of the Lord's new heaven—Michael, archangel of the skies; Gabriel, archangel of the land; and Raphael, archangel of the seas. When Lucifer arrives the next day, he is shocked to find the three angels sleeping there. Then he is even more horrified to see that the statue is wingless and nude; in his opinion, it is a disgusting image that doesn't resemble the Lord at all.

LUCIFER: Angels, what are you all doing? Sleeping on the job, are you?

MICHAEL: Sorry, your highness. The garden is very relaxing.

LUCIFER: And what is this disgusting statue? Where is the Lord God's statue?

Lucifer is interrupted by the Lord.

THE LORD: Lucifer, I see my statue has made it through the night.

LUCIFER: *Your* statue?

THE LORD: Yes. I shall call this one Adam. He is my greatest creation in this realm.

LUCIFER: A million pardons, my Lord, but where are its wings and halo?

THE LORD: This statue does not need wings or a halo. This statue is a human.

LUCIFER: Of course, it's human. I was simply putting the doubt in the ranks to rest. (*Lucifer glances at the archangels.*) Let all throughout the land know that the Lord God has made man. I say to you angels, prepare a feast for your God in celebration of this occasion.

All the heavenly beings prepare a great feast for the Lord God. Sundown comes, and the Lord returns to heaven.

At dawn, Lucifer checks on the garden. To his surprise, he finds a nude, wingless creature sleeping under the Tree of Life and Knowledge.

LUCIFER: What beast of the garden are thee? (*There is no response from the naked being.*) I say to you again, what beast of the garden are thee?

ADAM (*very startled*): I am Adam.

LUCIFER: Oh, the human. Well, I am Lucifer, the Lord's right hand. (*He throws a robe at Adam.*) Put on your angelic vestment. The Lord wants to see you today.

ADAM: Oh, thank you. I want to look my best for my creator.

LUCIFER: Then also clean the apple pieces off your face.

Just then, the Lord arrives in the garden; he embraces Adam, almost as father would a son.

THE LORD: Adam, my boy, let's take walk through the garden.

As they walk, the Lord and Adam talk about the wonders of the garden, the names the Lord has given to the creatures and plants of the land and sea, and about every inch of the garden's glory. Adam has one special subject on his mind.

ADAM: My Lord, the garden is a gift of which I am not worthy. But since you have given it to me, I do wish for one thing: a companion to help me enjoy it.

The Lord snaps his fingers, and the angel Lilith appears.

THE LORD: My boy, this is Lilith; your wish is her command. She shall accompany you on your travels through the garden. Well, my boy, it is sundown, and I must return to heaven. Sleep well; we will stroll through the garden again.

The Lord, accompanied by Lucifer, departs in his royal carriage, which is pulled by his beloved winged unicorns. Night comes, and the next day Adam and Lilith explore the garden's wonders. Adam does not realize that Lilith is a God-given servant and is comforted to have a companion. Lilith simply thinks she is doing the Lord's bidding.

ADAM: So, Lilith, are you enjoying the garden?

LILITH: Completely. Everything here is beyond earthly words.

ADAM: I know this is sudden, but would you stay here with me forever?

LILITH: What?

ADAM: We get along so well. We could have children. We could build a great life in the garden.

LILITH: First of all, you're not even an angel. Second, I don't want to have children with you. And third, no!

Offended, Lilith flies out of the Garden of Eden and back to heaven. Adam realizes that Lilith is one of the Lord's angel companions, nothing more. But his desire for a companion doesn't go away. He wants to spend time with someone, a human just like him. The following Sabbath the Lord returns to take another walk with Adam.

ADAM: My Lord, I hate to keep insisting on this, but I wish I had a companion I could live with forever.

LORD: I have a solution. I shall not only make you a companion, I shall make you a wife.

So, after dusk, the Lord gathers all of his angels and tells them they will make a woman for the man who inhabits their wonderful garden.

Part 2

The angels sing a beautiful and soulful song while the Lord and Lucifer prepare to make the woman. With the moon up above and the stars watching over all, the Lord waves his hand over Adam, and he falls into a deep sleep. The Lord takes one rib from the sleeping human. After he is done, there is a cross-shaped indent on Adam's right side. The Lord takes the rib over to a giant cauldron, where Lucifer is preparing all the ingredients to make the woman. In the cauldron are water, fire, sand, rose petals, a lock of angel hair, and finally the human rib. The Lord waves his hand over the cauldron, and a statue rises from within it. The Lord and Lucifer place the statue next to Adam, and Lucifer kisses the sleeping beauty, giving her the divine spark. Instantly, the being begins to breathe. The Lord sees what he has done and is pleased. And he, Lucifer, and all the heavenly hosts disappear into the mist of the morning dawn.

Dawn comes, bringing the next day. Adam wakes up and realizes that his wish has been granted. While Eve sleeps, he goes about his day. Eve wakes up just as he returns with food.

ADAM: Good morning.

EVE: Good morning.

ADAM: Are you hungry?

EVE: Sure. But first, I have one question. Who are you?

ADAM: I'm Adam. The Lord created me and placed me in this garden.

EVE: Okay ... I have another question. Who am I?

ADAM: You're Eve, and the Lord created you as well. I asked for a companion. Don't worry. I will explain everything today. Let's eat.

As they eat and interact, a wonderful calm enters the new world. They eat breakfast on the top of a hill that overlooks the entire garden. Nothing could be more perfect. Shortly after breakfast, they walk through the garden and come upon the Tree of Life and Knowledge. Lucifer is sitting in the tree, eating apples, pears, and oranges. Several snakes slither around the branches.

LUCIFER: So, this must Eve, the woman of the garden.

EVE: Yes, and you are?

LUCIFER: I am Lucifer, the Lord's second-in-command.

ADAM: Lucifer, what are you doing here?

LUCIFER: Just enjoying everything the garden has to offer.

ADAM: Why are you eating from this tree?

LUCIFER: This is the Tree of Life and Knowledge, the only tree from which I eat. This tree is for angels only.

ADAM: Does God eat from this tree too?

LUCIFER: Oh, yes, but he will tell you about that when he comes. Remember to wear your angelic vestments. You'll both want to look good for the Lord today.

Adam and Eve continue their walk. The Lord arrives shortly afterward, and the three of them walk through the garden.

ADAM: Eve and I saw Lucifer today, and he was sitting in the Tree of Life and Knowledge.

THE LORD: Neither of you ate from the tree, did you?

ADAM AND EVE (*together*): No!

THE LORD: Oh, good. That tree is forbidden to you. Terrible things will occur if you eat from it. Unnecessary evil will be the result. Stay far from that tree.

ADAM: We will, my Lord.

THE LORD: Adam and Eve, today has been just splendid. I cannot believe the dusk is here. I want you both to enjoy every gift of the garden. But remember not to eat fruit from the Tree of Life and Knowledge. Only the angels can eat from this tree. It is the only place in the garden where the angels can eat. My children, until we meet again, know that I love you always.

The Lord and Lucifer get into the royal carriage and fly back to heaven. Sundown comes. Many weeks pass, and the bond between the Lord and the humans grows stronger. Lucifer, however, still doubts the humans' purity and their overall purpose. One day, he sees Eve walking alone near the Tree of Life and Knowledge.

LUCIFER: Eve, my child, what are you doing here alone?

EVE: I am collecting fruit for Adam and myself.

LUCIFER: Well, the best fruit in the garden is on the Tree of Life and Knowledge. You have been in the garden long enough to know everything about the universe. The Lord feels temptation will come if you know too much. But I know that you and Adam both have the spark of the divine within you. So why would you be tempted?

EVE: To eat from the tree would be to betray our father. Adam and I cannot do it.

LUCIFER: Eve, I am God's child too, and I'm not evil. I eat of this tree, and it helps me understand and love my father more. You and Adam want to love God more, don't you?

EVE: Yes.

LUCIFER: Then take this fruit, share it with your husband, and no longer shall either of you live in the dark.

Adam and Eve spend the entire week eating fruit from the Tree of Life and Knowledge. They wait for the Lord to return so they can show him their knowledge of the light.

When the Lord returns on the Sabbath, he sees that Adam and Eve are covered in leaves. He is surprised that they are not wearing white as the angels do.

THE LORD: My children, why are you dressed in leaves and mud?

ADAM: Lucifer said we must be covered at all times, my Lord.

THE LORD: Who told you were nude?

EVE: Lucifer told us that if we ate from the tree, the truth would come to us.

THE LORD: How dare you listen to him and betray me. Get out of my garden. Wander about the wilderness from where you came, and never return to me until sin is gone from your soul.

The Lord opens the gates, and Adam and Eve leave the garden—not as images of God, but as humans who will never feel the divine spark again. The gates close behind them, and they are left to survive in the wilderness without the protection of God.

Part 3

The Lord turns to Lucifer, dismayed that his creations have turned against him.

THE LORD: Lucifer, what am I to do without my humans?

LUCIFER: Do not worry, my Lord. You can still watch them from heaven.

THE LORD: Who will protect them since I can't touch Earth?

LUCIFER: My Lord, let me be their guide. Let me show them that they are still your children.

THE LORD: You are forever looking out for what I need.

The Lord returns to heaven. Lucifer catches up with Adam and Eve in their new world. Adam and Eve do not know where to start, so Lucifer shows them that all they need to do is to follow the morning star, and they will never be lost. Lucifer shows them fire, tools, and how to hunt.

As time goes on, Adam and Eve have children and lead them and their descendants into the post-Eden era.

Eventually, the world becomes consumed by worldly things. Everywhere the Lord looks, there are images of Lucifer, constructed from materials from Lucifer's home in the heart of hell. Gold statues and false kings litter the world below. The Lord cannot have such things in the world that he loves so dear. So he saves one family and animals of every type (for animals were not guilty of human sin), and he floods the whole world. When Lucifer notices the water coming, he opens the gates of hell and ushers in every living soul who is not spared by the Lord. After forty days, the chosen family find themselves on Mount Ararat, from where they look down at the world reborn. The chosen people soon lead the world to redemption.

Chapter 2: A New Day

Part 1

As time goes by, the world moves on. The Lord's chosen people find themselves in a little town called Bethlehem. A humble couple has a son and stops to rest by the roadside before continuing their journey. Meanwhile, back in heaven, all the angels rejoice at the birth of the Lord's first son. The angels sing the very first Christmas hymn. As the festivities continue, the Lord notices that one face is not celebrating. It is Lucifer's; although he sings as loudly as the other angels, he also sarcastically praises God's new adventure.

LUCIFER: Oh, how I love to hear angels sing; it never gets old.

THE LORD: What are you doing here?

LUCIFER: I am here to congratulate your majesty on the birth of your son.

THE LORD: Thank you for the sentiment. You may leave now.

LUCIFER: Hey, is this the child who will fulfill the prophecy? The child who was to be born of a virgin, live, be crucified, and die, the one who was to descend to hell for three days and then return to the Lord's right hand on the third day?

THE LORD: Well …

Lucifer interrupts the Lord's thought, almost as though he has read his mind.

LUCIFER: No one knows? You didn't tell them the fate of this man? Well, I should go and see my competition up close. Good day to all. And again, my Lord, congratulations.

Lucifer goes down to Earth and offers the child a golden calf to wear around his neck. His mother, Mary, takes the gift, reluctantly and sadly, because she is one of the few who knows the fate of her child.

Part 2

Lucifer—careful not to let Jesus, the divine child, out of his sight—takes up residence in Galilee. He watches the child grow and get stronger and more powerful every day. One day, Jesus goes to the market with his parents, Joseph and Mary. They all stop to say hello to Lucifer.

JOSEPH: How is the shop doing, old man?

LUCIFER: Wonderful, couldn't be better. And how is young Jesus today?

JESUS: Fine, sir, thank you.

LUCIFER: Joseph, how are the boy's skills coming along?

JOSEPH: Very quickly; he learns fast. Jesus, stay here for one minute while I check out the other stands.

LUCIFER: Come here, child, let me show you a trick. Pour this water into this glass.

JESUS: Okay, now what?

LUCIFER (*grabs another glass*): Now pour the water into this one.

As Jesus pours, the water changes into wine.

JESUS (*in amazement*): Please do another trick.

LUCIFER (*picks up a rock from the ground*): What would you like this to be?

JESUS: A dove.

LUCIFER: Place your hand on the rock, close your eyes, and think of a dove.

A dove appears and flies away.

LUCIFER: Okay, that is enough for today. Now, run along and play.

Lucifer listens to Jesus talking to another boy as a group of children play in the street.

JESUS: Do not curse God, boy, or you shall become a pillar of salt.

YOUNG BOY: That will be the day.

Just then, the boy turns to salt. Lucifer runs into the middle of the crowd and throws his cape on the salt. When he whips it off, the boy is a boy again.

LUCIFER: The trick of the day for my favorite patrons.

The crowd applauds with approval. Lucifer takes the boy back to his shop.

LUCIFER: How do you feel, boy?

YOUNG BOY: Angry. I want to get back at that Jesus.

LUCIFER: No, my child, not now. Immediate revenge is no good. Hold on to your anger, and use it when the time is right. Child, what is your name?

YOUNG BOY: Judas.

Part 3

As time passes, Lucifer grows bored with Jesus. He tempts him in the desert; he tempts Jesus's followers. But nothing changes. So Lucifer has a new idea. He goes to talk to King Herod.

LUCIFER: Herod, king of the Jews, I have news of your future.

HEROD: You look like no angel I have ever seen. Who are you?

LUCIFER: I am Belial, Lucifer, Iblis.

HEROD: You look more like Beelzebub to me.

LUCIFER: Herod, a man called Jesus of Nazareth is going to take your throne. The people call him the king of Jews. Doesn't that worry you?

HEROD: Nonsense. The Hebrews are a simple people and have no idea whom they should adore.

LUCIFER: Herod, mark my words, this Jesus will soon become a problem for you.

Herod does not know what to believe. He is confused for days. Then the name Jesus keeps coming up in the court and among his advisors. He tells his staff to bring this Jesus to him and that he will decide the man's fate once and for all. Meanwhile, Jesus and twelve of his followers have supper together. Judas, the last to arrive, is stopped by Lucifer.

LUCIFER: Judas, are you ready for tonight?

JUDAS: Yeah. Where is my silver?

LUCIFER: Watch your tone with me, boy. Your silver is where I said it would be. Now, you promised me that you would make this happen.

JUDAS: I will.

LUCIFER: Don't toy with me, or I will rip your soul from bones. You will spend a million years in hell if this does not go right. Your God is counting on you to bring this man down. Now get in there and betray that impersonator.

Judas does so, and Jesus is brought before Herod to be judged. Herod, however, finds that no crime has been committed.

HEROD: Get this man away from my steps. He is not a criminal. He is a poor man, nothing more. This man has committed no crime against my crown. Send him to Pilate.

Chanting, "Pilate, Pilate!" the crowd takes Jesus to the Roman prefect's steps. Pilate comes out and is amazed at the chaos before him.

PILATE: Silence! Why do you Jews disturb me today and with such disrespect?

CROWD: Jesus must die! Jesus must die!

PILATE: Silence! What crime has this man committed?

CROWD: Blasphemy!

PILATE: Jesus, are you a god? Are you the king of the Jews, as rumors have it?

Jesus stands there, silent.

PILATE: This man says nothing. How can a mute and deaf man be a king? *(He addresses the crowd.)* I say to you, would you rather a murderer or Jesus be free?

CROWD: Barabbas! Barabbas! Barabbas!

PILATE: *(To his soldiers.)* Set Barabbas free. Still, I cannot condemn this man. I wash my hands of this problem. He belongs to the Jews now. Get this man away from my steps. *(He turns back to the crowd.)* May a curse come to you scribes, Pharisees, and rabbis if this man you wish to kill is just. Be gone, terrible crowd. Never come to my door again.

Lucifer watches all of this and whispers simultaneously in everyone's ears.

LUCIFER *(to Herod)*: Kill this man who calls himself "king of the Jews" and history will praise you.

LUCIFER *(to Pilate)*: Kill this man, and I will make you Caesar.

LUCIFER *(to Jesus)*: Show them you are God, and nothing more will happen to you. Paradise will be on Earth. Show them your power.

No one listens to Lucifer that day, and Jesus is killed on the cross.

Part 4

Three days after the chaos of the trial and crucifixion, Lucifer finds Jesus in his tomb. He watches Jesus stare at his own body lying before him. Lucifer emerges from the shadows.

LUCIFER: Jesus, it's time. Come with me.

They walk through the wall of the tomb and end up in Lucifer's office, which overlooks hell.

LUCIFER: Okay, Jesus, I have a deal for you. Tell me you are God, and we will go back up to Earth. You can rise from the dead on the Sabbath, and all will know that the Second Coming has occurred. Then, you will feel what I feel—power above all else.

JESUS: Do to me as you have done to my brothers.

Lucifer pauses for moment and looks at this sad man.

LUCIFER: Okay. Then you will be here for three days. You will be whipped one hundred times a day. Do you acknowledge the crimes you have committed? The crime of blasphemy. The crime of impersonating of a rabbi. The crime of fraternizing with a woman. Jesus, I sentence you to three days in hell. *(He turns to his assistants.)* Get him out of here.

Then a letter magically appears on Lucifer's desk. It is from the Lord and tells him to return to heaven immediately. Lucifer arrives to find an angry God.

THE LORD: One hundred whippings? Three days in hell? What are you doing to him?

LUCIFER: This is what is supposed to happen.

THE LORD: You will be …

LUCIFER: What? I will be what? This is your doing, not mine. Now I have two kingdoms to run. I say good day to you, my Lord.

Lucifer leaves heaven, realizing he has won the battle, but the war is far from over.

Chapter 3: Earth Has a New King

Part 1

Realizing that his dream will soon be realized, Lucifer decides that it is time for him and his newly wedded wife to be officially crowned as king and queen of the earth. Everything is ready; nothing is out of place. Lucifer and Lilith stand in front of the great temple and prepare to take the coronation oath that will forever tie them to the planet. Every person alive is there.

OFFICIANT: Lilith, please step forward. Are you ready to take your oath?

LILITH: Yes.

OFFICIANT: Place your hand on the holy texts and repeat after me. "I, Lilith do solemnly swear to protect the earth and all it contains. So help me God."

LILITH: I, Lilith, do solemnly swear to protect the earth and all it contains. So help me God.

OFFICIANT: Congratulations. Ladies and gentlemen, meet your new queen.

The crowd roars with excitement. Trumpets play, and a crown is placed upon Lilith's head.

OFFICIANT: Lucifer, please step forward. Are you ready to recite your oath as king of the earth and hell?

LUCIFER: Yes.

OFFICIANT: Proceed.

LUCIFER: I do solemnly swear a lot and plan to do whatever the hell I want when and how I want to do it. I will execute anyone I don't like. And to the best of my ability, I will preserve, protect, and defend my reputation as long as I live.

OFFICIANT: So help you God?

LUCIFER: So help me God!

OFFICIANT: Congratulations. Ladies and gentlemen, your king.

The crowd goes wild. Everyone heads to a great banquet and reception, the likes of which had never been seen before.

Part 2

Lilith and Lucifer arrive in a black carriage. They walk up to the head table as their names are announced.

ANNOUNCER: Ladies and gentlemen, the king and queen of the earth.

The first couple wave to their followers.

LUCIFER: People of Earth, tomorrow we battle, but tonight we indulge. So eat, drink, and be merry!

He gives his signature cackle and joins the dancing. The festivities continue, and then the announcer tells the king and queen that their troops are ready for inspection. It is the largest army in history. The demons march in perfect unison, and they salute the king and queen. Afterward, Lucifer leads Lilith to her new throne. He bows before his consort. He pauses for a moment and then kisses her cheek.

Meanwhile, the demons take the first family—Eve, Adam, and their son Cain—to the altar. Lucifer walks over to the first family.

LUCIFER: Who is the accused?

ANNOUNCER: This is Adam.

LUCIFER: Adam, am I your lord and savior?

ADAM: No!

LUCIFER: I'm not? Well, that's too bad because you're going to hell. Get him out of here. Who is the accused?

ANNOUNCER: Cain.

LUCIFER: Am I your lord and savior?

CAIN: Yes.

LUCIFER: Then bow to me, boy!

Cain bows down before his new king, hoping for a reprieve.

LUCIFER: Look at you, you swine. You would bow before just about anything. Get him out of here. Who is the accused?

ANNOUNCER: Eve.

LUCIFER: Eve? That curse upon humanity? The reason we battle God tomorrow? No longer shall you curse humanity. Instead, I put the curse on you. You shall you live on this planet until the end of time. You belong to the people now. *(He leans over and whispers into Eve's ear)*: Good luck with this crowd. I hear they can get angry. (*He pushes her into the crowd.*)

Part 3

The sun rises on an open field, which is lined with humans and demons on one side and the Lord's royal army on the other. David, who helped with Lilith and Lucifer's coronation ceremony, commands the angels in the hugest offensive ever seen.

DAVID: Angels, you are to not strike any human, only the fallen angels. You are all on God's mission now. Good luck and Godspeed!

On the other side of the field, Lucifer prepares his troops and the human fighters who have chosen to fight with him.

LUCIFER: Humans, your God has sent his angels to subdue you. I say, *never!* They have come to take your free will. I say, show them what free will is for! And remember, never fear death, even when it's looking you in the face. *(He turns to Lilith.)* My queen, on your signal, we fight for you.

LILITH: Beelzebub, you are free from your mortal binds.

All of a sudden, the largest, most demonic-looking beast arises. With the worst roar that was ever roared, Lucifer disappears, and Satan takes his place.

SATAN: Oh, it is so good to be free. Ha ha ha ha ha!

God's angels begin a full assault on Satan, who has no trouble fighting the weaker angels. Soon the Holy Ghost appears.

HOLY GHOST: Stand down, Satan.

Satan changes back into Lucifer.

LUCIFER: Your holiness, what a sad day to meet.

HOLY GHOST: Stop these silly magic tricks, and be redeemed.

LUCIFER: Magic tricks. You want to see magic? Get up, you lazy bums! Your master says rise!

Soon thousands of specters rise out of the ground.

LUCIFER: Your holiness, you have may have been able to fight the living, but try fighting the dead.

As the zombies march toward the Holy Ghost, the archangels appear to protect him. Lucifer walks away and is confronted by two archangels, Gabriel and Raphael.

RAPHAEL: Lucifer ... brother ... let us help you to redeem yourself.

LUCIFER: I will not accept redemption from traitors, and I am no longer your brother.

RAPHAEL: Forgive us, Lord, for what we are about to do. Come forth, Satan!

Lucifer transforms into the beast for a second time. As Satan, he fights Gabriel and Raphael with all his might and finally knocks them both to the ground. Then he becomes Lucifer again, only to find Michael standing there.

LUCIFER: Michael, what are you doing here?

MICHAEL: I'm here to set the beast free.

LUCIFER: What do you know of freedom? You are as bound as I am.

MICHAEL: Everyone wants freedom. Forgive me, Lord, for what I am about to do. Come forth, Satan!

Lucifer is transformed into Satan for the third and final time. By this time, the name Satan has been said twice. Two of the strongest beings in the universe battle with all their might. Satan knocks Michael to the ground and transforms back into Lucifer. He stands by as Raphael and Gabriel help Michael to stand up.

LUCIFER: Michael, I thought you were the left hand of God and I was just some little devil. What the hell happened?

GABRIEL: Sorry, my lord, but you became Satan.

LUCIFER: What did you just say? You have no idea what you have just done. You have unleashed the most powerful being in the entire universe. Do you feel my power? Do you cower beneath me? Do you fear the king of the earth?

MICHAEL: Devil, if you wish to be the king of the earth, then the earth is yours.

All of a sudden, Lucifer is shackled to the earth. It finally dawns on him that he has committed his first sin since falling from God's grace. All the light in his soul has left him.

LUCIFER: What is this? This isn't over. I will be back.

Then he bursts into flames and retreats to hell.

Chapter 4: Defeated

Part 1

After that terrible defeat, Lucifer arrives at the Garden of Eden to sign the Heaven and Hell Treaty. As he gets out of his carriage, the three archangels are there to greet him.

LUCIFER: I see that angels no longer salute their superiors.

MICHAEL: The Lord is waiting for you.

Lucifer enters the garden, where he signs the treaty. He realizes that he will no longer be an angel in grace, but he will be an angel with free will.

THE LORD: Well, my son, I have to go. Dusk is coming.

The Lord hugs Lucifer for the last time. Lucifer turns around and looks at the garden, also for the last time. Just as he is about to leave through the garden gates, he is stopped by the three angels.

MICHAEL: The Lord has something for you.

Gabriel hands Lucifer a package that contains a golden key. Raphael reads some words the Lord has written for Lucifer.

RAPHAEL: "This key allows you to always come back and look at the garden, but you will not be able to experience it in grace. Love always, Alpha and Omega."

Lucifer starts to tear up and continues walking through the gate.

MICHAEL: And, Lucifer, we will always salute a superior angel, even a fallen one.

Lucifer returns their salutes and walks away.

Part 2

The image of the garden fades into the background, and the scenery changes to a bustling metropolis. Lucifer disappears into the crowd. The lesson that he learns is not what sins to avoid or to stop committing, but never to fall away from love. Love conquers all, and only with love can everything be one and the same. Lucifer is destined to search for love forever so that someday he will be forgiven for his sins. But until then his pride will keep him away from anything close to love. He lives among humans as a temptation and a distraction. He loves to play games and make people think their hearts are talking when it is actually him.

Interlude: Lucifer's Return

After thousands of years of human existence, the devil fell by the wayside. As society progressed, God and Satan became smaller parts of everyday life. The people of the earth simply forgot about the realm up above. Things were so loosely managed by the beings up above that there was no need to make any waves; that is, until the issue of Armageddon was brought up for a vote conducted by the Universal Royal Council—God the Father, Jesus, and the Holy Ghost. The Virgin Mary was present but did not vote.

Also participating were the three archangels; the earthly representatives, Lilith, Adam, and Eve; and rulers of hell, Satan/Lucifer. Although Satan often showed up during the meeting, his vote never counted. The tie-breaker vote was held by Sir David, the speaker of the council. David never liked to talk about Armageddon because he did not want to have to break a tie. It was a tough choice, because God and Lucifer were never on the same side. Indeed, one particular council meeting would prove to be the start of a wild adventure, one that the earth would not forget.

The story began in the year 2000 of the modern era ...

Chapter 5: Armageddon

Part 1

As dawn rises over heaven, the council is a roundtable of supernatural power. Sir David brings the meeting to order.

DAVID: I open the floor for a discussion on the investigation into Armageddon.

The group is completely silent; no one responds.

DAVID: Since there is no debate, we will take an up-and-down vote. Simple majority wins. If there is a tie, I will vote to break it. Let's vote. Angels, how do you vote?

MICHAEL: We have three yes votes for Armageddon.

DAVID: Earth, how do you vote?

LILITH: We have three no votes for Armageddon.

DAVID: Heaven, how do you vote?

THE HOLY GHOST: We have one yes vote and one no vote for Armageddon.

DAVID: God, how do you vote?

THE LORD: Whichever way I vote, Lucifer will vote the opposite. I vote yes for Armageddon.

DAVID: Okay, Lucifer, the vote is five yeses and four no's. What is your vote?

LUCIFER: I feel that this vote today—like every other vote in history—is to show that our belief in the overall purpose of the earth and this great experiment is broken. I abstain from voting.

DAVID: Okay then, the investigation into Armageddon is approved by a simple majority. Congratulations to you all. If there is no new business, we are adjourned.

Everyone gets up and leaves the council.

DAVID: Lucifer, wait just a moment.

LUCIFER: Yes, Sir David?

DAVID: So, why would you give up your chance to make me do all the hard work and break a tie? There is no way you got a heart all of a sudden. There's no way you want to protect to humans, do you?

LUCIFER: David, what would I gain from this Armageddon investigation?

DAVID: Perhaps a chance to be the supreme commander of the angels' forces?

LUCIFER: Nothing God could say would make me command his army, but I'm sure you can do it.

David walks Lucifer to his carriage, and Lucifer gets in.

DAVID: I will find out what your angle is. You wait and see.

LUCIFER: Good day, Sir David.

Part 2

The next day, the Lord asks to see Lucifer in the garden. The two of them meet there regularly to discuss business items and sometimes have a lunch of fresh fruit and vegetables. On this particular day, however, the Lord has an agenda.

THE LORD: Lucifer, I'm so glad you could make it for lunch today.

LUCIFER: It's always a pleasure, my Lord.

THE LORD: So ... interesting vote on Armageddon the other day, no?

LUCIFER: Well, if it was what the Lord wished, then I am in accord.

THE LORD: I want this finished in forty days or less. Make a show for the angels up here and the humans down there. Everyone will be happy, and then we will return to normal.

LUCIFER: My Lord, you, yourself, ordered this to happen. If you would like me to do it, I will do so with full force, nothing less.

THE LORD: Just make examples of a few people and then let them go.

LUCIFER: As you wish, my Lord.

Lucifer leaves the garden and goes to speak with Lilith about how they might take over the earth. Lucifer and Lilith conclude that the media is the fastest way to get people's attention. So they assemble the biggest press conference that had ever been organized in the universe. Lucifer prepares by learning every language on Earth and every cultural nuance. He makes himself ready for television and radio. Down below is a scared human population, wondering what fate awaits them.

Part 3

A loud voice booms, "We are going live in five, four, three, two, one." The little red light turns on. Camera 1 is ready to film Lucifer giving his first worldwide address. Every human is glued to the radio, television, or Internet. People are nervous about what they are about to see and hear.

LUCIFER: Good afternoon, people of Earth. I know that you have all been anxious about my speech to you all today. I am here today to relay the news that the Lord God has decided that the entire human race will be investigated to see if the world has reached the point of Armageddon. Many steps must be taken, including an overhaul of human culture, a search for social balance, and an evaluation of so-called good people and so-called bad people. I need everyone to cooperate during this tough time, so that during the next forty days, the occupation of the earth goes smoothly. On the thirty-ninth day of the investigation, the Lord will decide whether to let the human race live or give the earth back to the angels. I have no more details at this time, but all will be informed as soon as I do. Thank you, and have a great day.

The studio goes dark. Lucifer disappears from sight and takes Lilith with him. People on Earth spend the next forty-eight hours discussing this most troubling news story. They are panicked by the idea that they have only forty days left. The Lord is not pleased at the way Lucifer released the news, but there is nothing he can do, since the process is already in motion. He maintains his faith in the human spirit, which he knows, deep down, is good.

Part 4

After his appearance on the global stage, Lucifer spends the next few days preparing to move from hell to the earth. Over the intercom, he hears, "Your highness, you have a visitor."

LUCIFER: Come in. Ah, David, to what do I owe this pleasure?

DAVID: I came to tell you that I no longer work for God.

LUCIFER: What?

DAVID: I resigned my post. I cannot sit by and let Armageddon happen without living on Earth at least once.

LUCIFER: Why did you come to hell first?

DAVID: You told me you wanted a chance to control part of the earth after the humans fail their test. And, my dear Lucifer, I want that too. Let me be your general, and we will end Armageddon in twenty days instead of forty.

LUCIFER: You expect me to betray the Lord a second time, especially now that judgment is so close? Are you insane? What could I possibly gain by listening to you?

DAVID: Your chance to be the god you always wanted to be. Once the humans are out of the way, only angels will be left on Earth. Angels don't have free will; they have to respect their superiors no matter what. With God in heaven and us on Earth, what will keep us from becoming gods among immortals?

LUCIFER: How dare you try to tempt me!

DAVID: Listen, your wife has been spending more time with God and less time with you. I overheard God telling Lilith to keep an eye on you.

LUCIFER: I won't listen to any more of this. Get out! Don't contact me again.

David leaves Lucifer's office, but Lucifer starts thinking about what he has said. David has started a train of thought that Lucifer is bound to make his own.

Chapter 6: Lilith's Loyalty

Part 1

After his meeting with David, Lucifer decides to test Lilith's loyalty. He finds her bathing in a hot spring, guarded by the archangels.

LUCIFER: Tell Lilith I am here to see her.

MICHAEL: I'm sorry, your highness. She is indisposed.

LUCIFER: I am her husband.

LILITH: Boys, it's okay. Give us a minute. *(The archangels leave.)*

LUCIFER: Lilith, why all the guards?

LILITH: We are occupying the earth; there is a chance of
      danger.

LUCIFER: Not for those who truly believe why we are
here.

Lilith gets out of the spring, walks over to Lucifer, and
kisses him, hoping to distract him from the business he's
come to talk about. But Lucifer has more of Satan's will
than his own. He will not succumb to the lusts of the
flesh.

LUCIFER: I have been getting daily reports about misconduct
      among your troops.

LILITH: It's true. What do you suggest we do?

LUCIFER: I want to make an example of one of the angels.
      I will not have disobedience in the ranks.

LILITH: Okay. Let's do it.

Lilith and Lucifer gather all the troops and call up one of
the angels who had committed sin on Earth.

LILITH: You, angel, what is your rank?

ANGEL: Captain.

LILITH: Captain, it has been brought to my attention that you and others in your unit enslaved some of the humans in your sector. Is this true?

ANGEL: Yes, your highness.

LILITH: Well, Captain, every angel in your troop who enslaved a human will be de-winged and drowned. And, Captain, your punishment is to watch the torture and to make sure everything goes smoothly, I want you to report back to me directly when the deed is completed. *(Lilith turns to the others in the crowd.)* To the rest of you, I say, hell is where you will go if any more crimes are committed. Now, get out my sight, all of you.

Lucifer was pleased, but he still did not know if Lilith was on his side or God's.

Part 2

The council members hold an emergency meeting to discuss the Armageddon investigation. Worry and fear are starting to spread, and even the Lord cannot stop the chaos. Finally the Lord calls the group to order. He reassures everyone that everything will work out; as long as they maintain control of the investigation, no catastrophes will happen. All of sudden, there is a flash of light, and Lucifer appears, dressed as a supreme commander.

LUCIFER: What is going on here?

THE LORD: We are meeting about what do about the occupation of Earth.

LUCIFER: I am the supreme commander of the angels and the demons. I should have been included.

THE LORD: We all figured you were busy, and we planned to tell you everything later.

LUCIFER: I don't believe you. In any case, I'm going back to Earth to speak to the people about all the new restrictions being imposed on them.

THE LORD: You can't do that!

LUCIFER: Oh, are you taking away my free will?

THE LORD: Well, no ...

LUCIFER: Good. Guards, take his majesty back to heaven where he belongs.

The guards remove a reluctant God and put him in his carriage.

LUCIFER *(turns back to the council)*: The rest of you are in violation of the Heaven and Hell Treaty. Get comfortable. You are going to be here for a long time. No one is allowed to leave. The land of Eden is now under hell's control.

LILITH: Lucifer, what about me?

LUCIFER: I am glad you asked that question. Lilith, you are no longer my general. David, you are now my second-in-command.

Lucifer and David leave the garden to prepare Lucifer for his second speech to the world.

Part 3

A voice booms over a loud speaker: "Your majesty, you go live in five, four, three, two, one." The red light comes on.

LUCIFER: People of Earth, I am addressing you tonight because we have reached the point of no return. Four rebel forces from around the globe have united and declared war on me. Declaring war on me is the same as declaring war on God himself. So, to the rebels, I say you have nine days to prepare to fight. The battlefield will be the holiest land on Earth, the Valley of Freedom. All individuals who do not participate in the war shall not be judged by God. These are Earth's final days. Make choices that will last an eternity, for after the fortieth day that is all we will have. Good luck to all, and Godspeed to everyone.

The light goes out, and Lucifer disappears into the darkness.

Chapter 7: Lucifer Dies So Satan Can Live

Part 1

The Lord comes down to the garden to speak with Lilith.

THE LORD: Lilith, I have an idea about how to save Earth.

LILITH: How?

THE LORD: I will give you the golden dagger to strike Lucifer in the heart and separate Lucifer from Satan once and for all. Separating the two will give Lucifer a chance to think clearly.

LILITH: But how can we ensure that happens?

THE LORD: Easy. I will demand that you fight on the human side. I asked him to meet me here today. Here he comes.

LUCIFER: Okay, what was so pressing?

THE LORD: I want Lilith to fight on the human side.

LUCIFER: Why?

THE LORD: I know she is the only one you will not harm.

LUCIFER: Okay, she is free to go. But only for this fight, and then she is to come right back here.

Lucifer lets Lilith go, and she helps the humans organize for their battle against him.

Part 2

As dawn comes over the valley, both sides prepare for battle. First, the leaders of each side meet to set up the ground rules. Lucifer and Lilith agree to a clean fight. As they walk away, Lucifer leans over to David.

LUCIFER: Whatever you do, do not let Lilith near me. Whatever she and God have planned will not be good for me. *(He turns to his army.)* Let the battle begin!

With a demonic roar, the fighting starts. Lucifer, stronger than ever, slays tons of humans at once. Meanwhile, Lilith and David battle each other to see who will be Lucifer's second-in-command. Lilith has a stroke of luck; she takes a cheap shot and knocks David out cold. She then looks for Lucifer so she can kill him.

LILITH: You're dead, boy!

LUCIFER: Bring it on, little girl! *(He roars.)*

The two fight like no two beings on Earth have fought before. Finally, with one good thrust of his sword, Lucifer knocks Lilith to the ground. As he goes in for the kill, she stabs him with the Lord's golden dagger. The battle stops, and everyone realizes that the devil is dying. Lilith holds Lucifer as he dies.

LUCIFER: Lilith ...

LILITH: What? *(She starts to cry.)*

LUCIFER: I feel so cold.

Lucifer dies, and the spirit of Satan is freed. It flies into the nearest body—David's.

DAVID: Let it be known throughout the land, the king of hell has met his end!

Everyone bows as Lucifer's body is carried back to the Garden of Eden for all eternity.

Chapter 8: Once Again, We Have Balance

All of heaven's beings are celebrating in excitement. Lilith stands next to the Tree of Life and Knowledge. She has mixed feelings about the earth's success in battle. She had lost her beloved, even though she saved her treasured humans and her earthly kingdom. The Lord comes to her side.

THE LORD: Lilith, my dear, why aren't you celebrating?

LILITH: I miss Lucifer. I know I had to kill him, but he was my husband.

THE LORD: Well, the great thing about being divine is that only your body dies, never your spirit.

LILITH: You mean he is still here?

THE LORD: In his favorite place.

The Lord walks away, and Lucifer comes out from behind the Tree of Life and Knowledge. Lilith is overjoyed to be reunited with her husband, the one with whom she fell in love. She hugs and kisses him.

LUCIFER: My dear, you didn't actually think I would let you kill me completely, do you?

LILITH: I didn't know what would actually happen.

LUCIFER: It's good to be back to my old self again. Come on. I hear Jesus is two thousand years old today, and you know how much I love birthday cake.

Heaven and Earth rejoice again as balance returns to the universe. Even Satan and his new master David join in the worldwide party.

Interlude: A Girl, a Crystal, and Fate

A long time ago, long before the world was as it is, Lucifer, light bearer and the morning star, created a duplicate devil out of crystal. He did this so he would have a backup, if the Lord God tried to destroy him.

This crystal became more and more useless as time went on. Lucifer/Satan gained control of hell and most of the earth. God sat in heaven, bound by the law of free will. As such, there was no need for the crystal. In addition, Lucifer, without realizing it, had lost the crystal some four billion years earlier. But it was only a matter of time before this otherworldly object would surface.

When a young archaeologist named Sara stumbled across this artifact, she had no idea of its power and history. Everything from beginning to end was held in that crystal; it was almost a mini-tree of life and knowledge.

All the world's secrets were held tightly inside, including a duplicate Lucifer. The danger was the crystal might fall into the wrong the hands; if so, that individual could start the world over again and become the new god.

Sara, however, believed she had found another archaeological artifact and put the crystal on the display at an exhibition in Canada. All of the foremost scholars and scientists of the day were present at the unveiling of her discovery. What Sara did not know was that certain other guests had shown up too.

Chapter 9: A Young Girl's Bad Dream

Part 1

As all the experts from around the world enjoy the exhibition, Sara stares at the ruby-red crystal. It is glowing with an intense and wonderful, out-of-this-world light. She is deep in thought about where the object came from when she is interrupted by David, who admires the crystal as well.

DAVID: My dear, what a wonderful find you have made.

SARA: Oh, you startled me.

DAVID: A thousand apologizes, my dear. No harm intended. I am simply an admirer of archaeological artifacts.

SARA: This one is like nothing I have ever seen before. It almost seems divine in nature; it shines and glows as if it has never been touched.

DAVID: Yes, it does seem otherworldly. What will happen to it when the exhibition is over?

SARA: It will go into my private collection, I suppose.

DAVID: My dear, let me take it off your hands ... for a handsome price, of course.

SARA: Well ...

Just then Lilith joins them.

LILITH: I see you have found my crystal. David, thank you, I will take it with me now.

DAVID: Over my dead body.

LILITH: Don't tempt me, because that can be arranged.

Lilith and David are interrupted as Satan slips out of David's body and manifests himself in human form for the first time.

SATAN: No one is going anywhere with that crystal. It is mine.

To everyone's surprise, Lucifer appears.

LUCIFER: Am I interrupting something?

DAVID: What are you doing here?

LUCIFER: I have every right to that crystal. I'm the one who created it.

DAVID: It is an artifact of hell. It belongs to me.

LILITH: It has been on Earth for millennia. It belongs to me.

SARA: Um, I'm the one who found it.

LUCIFER: Shut up! *(He turns to Satan.)* Slave, tell them to whom the crystal belongs.

SATAN: I am sorry, my Lord, but you too must fight for the crystal.

LUCIFER: So be it.

Lucifer turns over a table and pushes David against the wall. He and Lilith are the first two to battle over the crystal. Lucifer pins Lilith in a corner, thrusts his sword into her, and she disappears. David screams.

DAVID: Lucifer, I'm going to kill you!

LUCIFER: Why would you fight me first and let the girl get away with the crystal?

DAVID: Oh, good point.

LUCIFER: Of course it is, you idiot.

The two of them turn to Sara and back her into a corner.

DAVID: I wonder, since we're in Canada, if she bleeds maple syrup.

LUCIFER: Forget the syrup, you moron. I bet she tastes like Canadian bacon. Come here, little girl, come to Uncle Lucifer.

At the last minute, Lucifer turns and thrusts his sword into David.

LUCIFER: That's for saying you were going to kill me.

David disappears, and Lucifer turns to Sara.

LUCIFER: Sorry if I frightened you, my dear, but I couldn't let him kill you.

LUCIFER *(turns to Satan and screams his slave name)*: Genie Du Mal!

SATAN: Yes, your Majesty?

LUCIFER: Get the crystal, and let's go.

SATAN: My Lord, I cannot. Sara is my new master.

LUCIFER: What? There isn't anywhere you can hide the girl. I know every inch of the universe.

Satan puts the crystal on a chain and places it around Sara's neck.

LUCIFER: Well good luck in the cold, I'm not the only demon to be afraid of.

Lucifer disappears in a fiery blaze. And then demons appear and circle Sara and Satan, chasing them out of the building and into hell.

Part 2

After he lets Satan escape with Sara, Lucifer thinks about how to retrieve the girl. He calls on Adam, Eve, and Lilith to help him kidnap her and take her out of hell.

ADAM: What's the plan?

LUCIFER: All of us are invited to the king of hell's annual celebration at court. Adam and Eve will wear traditional human garments, similar to what Sara is likely to have on. Lilith, you and I, will wear our royal garments. As the evening progresses, Sara and Eve will switch places, and I will take the girl out of hell.

LILITH: Why isn't David here?

LUCIFER: The less he knows, the more likely it is for this plan to succeed.

All of them head to the ball. The minute that Lucifer walks in, he notices that Sara is sitting on a royal throne on a stage in front of the crowd. She is dressed just as he knew she would be. Next to her sits David and next to him, preparing for the show, is Satan.

SATAN: Let the dance begin!

SARA: What are they doing?

DAVID: They are dancing the traditional *Guerra*.

SARA: You mean the legendary dance between hell's demons and humans?

DAVID: Yes.

Soon, everyone is dancing. Lilith, Lucifer, Adam, and Eve begin the routine they'd rehearsed to distract David and Satan. Adam, Eve, and Lilith dance and captivate the audience. Lucifer finds Sara and places a veil over her face, similar to one that Eve has over her face, and sneaks Sara out the front door. They slip out of hell and into the Garden of Eden.

Part 3

Several days later, Lucifer is working in garden. He is visited by Sir David.

SECRETARY: Your highness, Sir David is here to see you.

LUCIFER: Send him in.

David enters wearing his angel's military apparel.

LUCIFER: To what do I owe this disgusting pleasure?

DAVID: Sorry to bother you, your highness. Word has it that you know where the girl is.

LUCIFER: What business is it of yours?

DAVID: I am simply trying to help you retrieve the crystal.

LUCIFER: I need no help at all.

DAVID: I want to retrieve the crystal for our redemption.

LUCIFER: What do you mean "our" redemption? I am divinely created, so redemption is inevitable for me.

DAVID: Sorry, when I said our redemption, I meant Lilith's and mine.

LUCIFER: Well, that is very thoughtful, except Lilith is God's chosen protector of Earth, so redemption is inevitable for her as well.

DAVID: Fine! I want the crystal for my own redemption and to ensure my place in history.

LUCIFER: You are the king of hell. You are in history.

DAVID: I was ousted by Satan when my plan to get the crystal from Sara didn't work. Now, I am an angel without a place in the universe.

LUCIFER: I should laugh at your misfortune, but for some reason I cannot do to you what you have done to me. At dawn tomorrow, report to Lilith, and she will tell what your new position will be. Now, get out here.

DAVID: You are gracious, your highness ...

LUCIFER: Out!

David leaves immediately, but the silence around Lucifer is short-lived.

SECRETARY: Your highness, you have a call from the Lord.

LUCIFER: Okay, put it through.

THE LORD: Lucifer, my boy, how are you?

LUCIFER: I'm fine, my Lord. To what do I owe this pleasure?

THE LORD: I was wondering why there is a human in my garden.

LUCIFER: It was the only place I could keep the girl safe until I could figure out what to do with her.

THE LORD: Well, she can't stay there. So get her out or something terrible will happen. You have until the end of today. Talk to you later, Lucifer.

LUCIFER: Okay, my Lord.

Lucifer goes to find Sara and get her out of the garden.

Chapter 10: Hide Them Both

Part 1

In no time at all, Lucifer finds Sara sitting next to the Tree of Life and Knowledge. She looks tired and confused, unaware of where she is. Lucifer walks up to her.

LUCIFER: Sara, child. What's wrong?

SARA: I have no idea what is going on. Why is everyone after this crystal?

LUCIFER: It's complicated.

SARA: I've got time. Tell me!

LUCIFER: The crystal is both a complete copy of me and a portable Tree of Life and Knowledge. It holds all the secrets of the universe. The person who has it has the same power as God himself. Everyone in the universe wants that crystal so he or she will not be judged by God. People believe that if they give the crystal to God first, then they will be spared from judgment. Since it is around your neck, you are the one with all the power.

SARA: I don't want it anymore.

LUCIFER: Well, I guess you could give it to ...

Before he can finish his thought, an angel runs over to Lucifer.

ANGEL: Your highness, demons are attacking the garden. Lilith and David are out there, but they cannot hold them off for long.

Lucifer tells Sara to stay there and wait for him or Lilith to come for her. He flies over the garden wall and lands next to Lilith and David.

DAVID *(shouting)*: Demons! Stand down!

LUCIFER: How is the diplomacy working?

DAVID: Not well.

LUCIFER: If either of you get captured, struggle with them. Don't go willingly.

With a big roar, Lucifer flies toward the demons. David and Lilith begin to bombard them with light bombs, which explode and produce tons of light, frying the demons. The three fight with all their combined strength. Lucifer grabs Lilith from behind and throws her over the garden wall.

LUCIFER: You two, get the girl out of the garden.

The demons pounce on Lucifer with their full strength. Lucifer throws the demons off him and flaps his wings, sending several demons flying away. There are thousands of demons, fighting with all their might against their former leader.

On the other side of the wall, Lilith finds Sara.

LILITH: Sara!

SARA: Oh, thank God.

LILITH: Girl, we've got to get you out of here. If you keep that crystal around your neck, no one can harm you.

Lilith opens the door to Limbo and pushes Sara through.

LILITH: Good luck, child, and Godspeed.

DAVID: Lilith we've got to go. Lucifer needs our help.

David and Lilith jump over the top of the wall. They see that Satan and the demons have surrounded Lucifer.

DAVID: We're too late.

The demons tackle Lucifer to ground, and Satan walks up to him.

SATAN (*to Lucifer*): You are not as powerful when you are bound in chains, are you?

LUCIFER: I will always be more powerful than you are. I am not a coward!

Satan smacks Lucifer across the face.

SATAN: Get him up.

LUCIFER: You are all traitors. God will punish you for this.

SATAN: Gag him! Chain him! And bring him along!

The demons chain his feet. They tie his arms behind his back to keep his wings from flapping. They put a chain around his neck and a mask on his face. Lucifer is completely harmless. They drag him through the gates of hell. He struggles the whole way down. Lilith and David stand by. They can do nothing but let the demons take Lucifer away.

Part 2

After Lucifer spends three days in the heart of hell, Lilith confronts Satan.

LILITH: What are you going to do with Lucifer?

SATAN: Since you sent the girl with the crystal into Limbo, I am going to send Lucifer there to punish you. If the crystal is going to be destroyed, Lucifer may as well go with it.

Satan and Lilith walk to the altar.

SATAN *(screaming)*: Bring the beast!

Lucifer is completely bound, and the demons make him kneel before the altar. They rip off Lucifer's shirt, and Satan takes a cold brand to Lucifer's demonically warm body and burns the words *l'oscurita per simper,* meaning "darkness forever," on Lucifer's chest. To further embarrass him, they brand his left arm with a crescent moon to remind him that he will never be full or right again. Then the demons put on his angelic robe and push him into the light of Limbo.

Chapter 11: The First Time God Saw Her

Lucifer and Sara sit at huge, long table. Otherwise, the room is completely empty. Lucifer folds his hands and bows his head.

SARA: What are you doing?

LUCIFER: I am meditating.

SARA: Why?

LUCIFER: We are sitting in Limbo, about to be judged by God, and I am taking this moment to put my thoughts in order.

SARA: You are Lucifer. Don't you know your fate already?

LUCIFER: Even I have to pray for grace and mercy.

SARA: You are kidding, right?

LUCIFER: My dear, I may know my fate, but I still need mercy.

SARA: Well, I don't need anything or anyone. I have always been alone. I have no reason to repent.

LUCIFER: Your pride and pessimism are keeping you from understanding anything, you stupid human.

SARA: Hey, you're the one who is stupid if you think God will forgive the devil. You have no idea what is like to be completely alone. You will never understand being the only one who is burdened with the power of the universe.

LUCIFER: Now you know how God feels all the time. Child, you have had this crystal on your neck for just a few days. God has had that power forever. Now think about his loneliness after I fell from grace, and yet he can find mercy even for me. Maybe now that you are in God's position, you should let yourself feel what is real and not hold on to anger.

The door opens. Lucifer and Sara walk through it and are back in the Garden of Eden.

Chapter 12: How Satan Got Free Will

Once they realize they are back in the garden, Lucifer and Sara are stunned to see how it looks. It is almost as though a heavenly being is present. The fog clears, and Sara sees Jesus, the Holy Spirit, and the Virgin Mary. To the left are the three archangels and next to them, Adam and Eve. Sara is overwhelmed with emotion as she stares at the holy group in front of her. The crystal around her neck finally stops glowing. She turns to Lucifer to ask why and realizes that David, Lilith, and Satan are standing next to him. God motions for her to come toward him.

THE LORD: My child, there is no need to be shy.

SARA: I don't know ... what to ...

LUCIFER: Sara, give him the crystal.

Sara looks at Lucifer and nods her head. She is unable to speak. Lucifer helps her take off the necklace. She starts to hand the crystal to the Lord.

THE LORD: I cannot accept what is not mine. Give the crystal to its creator, Lucifer.

Sara turns to Lucifer and hands him the crystal.

LUCIFER: I cannot accept it either. It belongs to Satan

THE LORD: Satan if you accept this crystal, you are accepting free will and all the responsibility that goes with it.

Satan takes the crystal, stunned to realize he not only has all the power in the whole world, he also has a conscience. He is confused and relieved for the first time in his life. The garden fades away, and Sara finds herself back in the exhibition hall. God and Lucifer are standing next to her, looking at the crystal inside its glass case. It is not glowing.

LUCIFER: Sorry about all the chaos. I hope we didn't ruin your big night.

SARA: You both have opened my eyes to something I wasn't completely sure about. I feel like every question has been answered, every doubt has been erased, everything in the world is at peace.

THE LORD: My dear, everything you feel, you experienced through your heart. Child, go and help others find what their hearts are telling them. Go and enjoy your party. You are the main event.

Sara hugs the Lord and Lucifer and then goes back to the reception.

THE LORD: Well, Lucifer, my boy, it is always a pleasure. For some reason, I'm going to miss you.

LUCIFER: My Lord, I'm sure we'll meet again.

The two deities shake hands and disappear. Sara hosts one of the best receptions of the twenty-first century, and balance is returned to the universe.

Epilogue: Love and Peace at Last

And so it was that Satan got his freedom. Although he shared his kingdom with Lucifer and Lilith, he still had most of the responsibility. Satan had coveted freedom for so long, but what he did not realize was that freedom came with a price. With freedom came conscience, and with a conscience came the idea that soon he would be judged, just like everyone he tempted. He also experienced emotions, all of them, including love.

In Satan's eyes, nothing was more important than freedom and free will. But when he was finally given what humans live with every day, he became what he never wanted to be—mortal. That is the great thing about being human— we accept the responsibility that accompanies free will and love, because we know that redemption is always close by and that love truly does conquer all. As long as you never stray far from love, life will always be free.

About the Author

Jessy King was born in Omaha, Nebraska, on October 7, 1983. His birth name was Jesse Enrique Mata. When he finished grade school, he moved to Corvallis, Oregon. After high school, he participated in a student exchange program in Italy, where he fell in love with languages, writing, reading, music, and art.

When Jessy returned to the United States in late 2002, he attended Oregon State University, working at odd jobs throughout the Mid-Valley. In 2004 and 2005, he was chosen to play a king in a local theater production of a musical pantomime version of Cinderella. All around town he was nicknamed "Jessy the King Mata." Over time, that nickname was shortened to Jessy King, which is the name he uses today.

In late 2009 Jessy found his creative spark when he started writing *The Greatest Fall from Grace*. The inspiration came after Jessy went to his first Bible study meeting. He decided to put what he'd learned into story form. After months of writing and rewriting, Jessy created a story in which the theme and moral had the same focus: eternally divine and gracious love. Slowly, the story took shape until it was finally complete.

Words are tools that must be used only for the progression of society and never for the regression of humanity.

—Jessy King